The Empty Swing

The story of a child lost

by
Belinda Conniss

Cover illustration by C.R. McCool

Photography by S. Michaela McCool

I would also like to thank Kim Kimber

(www.kimkimber.co.uk)

for copy-editing *The Empty Swing*

Contents

Introduction

1972, London, England, Elizabeth McDaid, aged 18, was working for the *Times* newspaper.

Elizabeth came from humble beginnings, in Simi Valley, USA. Her father, a farmer's son, originally from Donegal, Ireland, and her mother, a seamstress, left the US for London in 1964 when Elizabeth was just ten years old.

Elizabeth was a quiet girl who felt that she didn't belong in London and, throughout her school years, she was rather reserved. Her mother and father were private people and very protective of her.

Of course, she had friends but her parents didn't allow Elizabeth to mingle outside of school. She had studied hard to get where she was today, and enjoyed her job, but it wasn't enough. Elizabeth always felt there were bigger and better things that she could be doing, and she had a yearning to travel.

Elizabeth had this empty feeling and a recurring dream, or what she believed to be a dream, of her sitting on a swing and someone else on a swing next to her. Although she was aware that there was someone sitting on the other swing, she never did see a face.

Elizabeth missed her home in Simi Valley and so, one day, at dinner, she told her parents that she wanted to go back to Simi for a holiday to visit relatives. There was a look of shock on her parents' faces and they immediately said no.

They told her that there were no relatives left in Simi, which Elizabeth found rather strange because she knew that her mother had been receiving letters from back home on a regular basis. However, Elizabeth dropped the subject when she realised that the thought of her going back there seemed to upset her parents.

Then, four years later, Elizabeth again decided to tell her parents that she was going back. An opportunity had arisen at work that would take her to Calabasas to cover a story in relation to the 'Pumpkin Festival'. Elizabeth figured that, as she would be in the area, she may as well go back and relive some childhood memories.

Back in Simi, however, she realised exactly why her parents didn't want her to return and, God knows, they tried hard to persuade her to decline the offer that her employers were keen for her to accept.

Once in Simi, Elizabeth began to unravel the truth about why they had left. Should she stay or leave? How did her parents explain the unusual, yet bazaar, set of circumstances that led to them leaving the valley? And just who was sitting on the other swing?

Chapter 1

I felt a little guilty that I was to spend a month away from home but, at the same time, I was quite excited when the day came to pack my case ready to travel.

In a sense, I felt a kind of achievement that I had worked so hard to one day be able to return to my roots, something that my parents were against from the very start.

On several occasions, I would hear my parents in their room discussing how they could persuade me not to go, although I only ever heard snippets of the conversation because I didn't want to disrespect them by being caught listening at the door.

A couple of weeks before I was due to travel, I sat down with my mother, while my father was at work, and asked her, "Why? Why is it so terrible for me to go home to Simi?"

My mother simply said, "We would rather you didn't go back! How could you possibly remember your life there? You were only ten when we moved to London."

My mother went on to tell me a story of how her grandparents left Ireland when she was a baby and how she couldn't remember anything about Ireland.

"Yes," I said, "but that was such a long time ago, obviously you wouldn't be able to remember. Why did your parents decide to move to the States in the first place?"

"Times were very hard," she explained. "They were extremely poor and my father was given such a wonderful opportunity it made sense for them to move. My parents were farm immigrants. It was quite tough, they moved to Boston and many immigrants had taken to cleaning yards and stables, unloading ships, and pushing carts to make a decent living.

"After some time, my parents moved to Simi Valley. I loved it but your father wanted to come home."

"So, why did we end up here in England?" I asked, "Why not back to Ireland?"

"Well, your father thought it would be better to move here as things, even now, are still pretty tough in Ireland. A lot of people from Ireland are having to take jobs elsewhere to make a good wage.

"Besides," said my mother, "you say you want to go back home? London is your home. There is nothing back in Simi for you, we don't have any relatives there anymore and most of the industry in the surrounding areas has gone, so there is nothing to see, or do, come to that."

I got the impression that my mother was trying to put me off. Next thing, the door opened and it was my father. He must have heard some of the conversation because he said, in an angry voice, "Tell them to send somebody else, I forbid you to go back."

I was quite upset and shocked that my father had raised his voice, it wasn't something he had ever done before. I left the room. I was sure that the sadness could be seen on my face as I lay on top of my bed to gather my thoughts.

After some time, I decided I was going and that was that, how could I possibly give up such an opportunity?

I went into work the day before I was due to leave and gathered all the paperwork I needed for my trip. The project in Calabasas was to interview local people about the history of the Pumpkin Festival.

I just couldn't wait to get there, mainly because I would be able to visit Simi as I was going to be there for one month.

Deep down, I also felt I had to get to the bottom of my recurring dream. There was something about the dream that involved Simi, and I was determined to know what it was.

I had never told my parents about the dream. I didn't feel that they would understand, because I didn't understand it myself.

Things were a little frosty between me and my parents. They seemed disappointed in me and couldn't bring themselves to talk to me once I had made up my mind that I was going.

I arrived at the port in Southampton, on 27 May 1976, ready for my journey to Quebec on the *Empress of Britain*. I had been waiting for this moment for a long time and it gave me a feeling of independence. I was still a little sad that my parents didn't approve, nor did they see me off.

My father went to work as normal and my mother was still in bed when I left. Was it because I left at six thirty in the morning? Or was it because she couldn't bring herself to talk to me? I guess I may never know.

On the boat I made myself comfortable for the long journey ahead. I had taken a book to read but I couldn't concentrate as guilt started to edge its way into my thoughts, was I doing the right thing?

Soon, I drifted off to sleep, but it wasn't long before I woke, feeling a little scared, sweat pouring from my face. The dream seemed to be more prominent and, this time, I could see the back of a child's head on the other swing, but still no face.

After a short time, I fell back asleep and there was no dream this time, just a relaxed, much-needed rest with no thoughts of anything that made me miserable.

I felt this sudden rush of emotion as I stepped off the boat, on arrival in Quebec five days later, happy that I was now closer to the place I still thought of as home.

I was met at the port and driven to Rue Sainte-Anne, to the Clarendon Hotel. Once I stepped into the foyer of the hotel I gasped, I couldn't believe just how beautiful it was, and was extremely happy that my boss had paid for my travel and the hotel. It was something that I definitely couldn't afford on my own.

The hotel was filled with grandeur and beautiful pictures of the rich and famous hung on the walls. The carpet was a deep red with not a mark on it and even the surrounding decor looked like it was brand new.

As I checked in, I commented on how clean and beautiful the hotel was, "You must have extremely hardworking staff here? I have never seen a place look so clean."

"Why, thank you, Madam," said the receptionist.

My room was out of this world, from the furnishing right down to the accessories in the bathroom, and I felt like a princess, only there was no prince. I had never had a boyfriend. Sure, I had had male companions, but not of the romantic type. In a way, I felt my parents wouldn't approve of a boyfriend unless he was someone that wanted to marry me.

I did, however, want to save myself for Mr Right! In my line of work, I've come across many men who liked the ladies and they would often travel on business and take their mistress with them. I didn't want to be that wife who stayed at home while my husband travelled for work with another woman on his arm.

My boss, Mr Greaves, was one of those men. His wife knew that he had a mistress but there was nothing she could say or do, and, indeed, a lot of couples lived that way. Once, I asked Mrs Greaves why she allowed this. Her reply was, that when you were kept in the sort of lifestyle she had, you put up with it.

Times were hard and many people lived such poor lives that to be in a marriage that provided was not to be sniffed at. Besides, if Mrs Greaves didn't allow it, it would be back to scrubbing floors for a living. That conversation made me think of how fortunate I was to be living with my parents and being able to save money so that when I did eventually marry, I would still have some form of independence.

As I had two days in Canada before I had to travel to Calabasas, I decided to take a trip to the little monastery town of Sainte-Anne-de-Beaupré situated on the banks of the St Lawrence River.

The Catholic Church has credited St. Anne with many healing miracles, and that has made the Basilica of Sainte-Anne-de-Beaupré a huge draw for pilgrims.

I couldn't help thinking of my parents when I was there, my father from an Irish Catholic background would have loved to have had the opportunity to visit such a beautiful church, as would my mother.

I got talking to the local tour guide, after spending several hours there, who said that, if I had enjoyed it so much, I should also visit 'Scala Santa'.

"Now that," she told me, "is breathtaking." I thanked her and said I would try to visit.

The next morning, after breakfast, I went there but I didn't expect to be so overcome with emotion. The Scala Santa Chapel (Chapel of the Holy Steps) was built in 1871. The steps replicate the stairs that Christ climbed when he was taken before Pontius Pilate.

Canada was beautiful and, right then, I promised myself that one day I would return. I walked along the river path while taking in the quaintness of it all. I soon came across a little art gallery with a cafe at the back where I could sit and have lunch.

While taking the tour of the gallery I couldn't help notice a young man looking in my direction. I tried to avoid his glare and carry on, but as soon as I moved to the other side he was right there.

With my head down, I quickly walked to the cafe and ordered lunch, I thought it better to eat then continue the tour.

A short while later, the man came into the cafe and ordered himself a coffee, then proceeded to sit three tables from mine.

The waitress came over with his coffee and he thanked her, then he looked at me and said, "Excuse me, I have to say, I have a feeling that I know you?"

"No," I replied, "I don't think so, I'm sure if I knew you I would recognise you."

"My mistake," he said, "You look like someone I know but just can't think who."

The man introduced himself as Bernard and asked me my name, then he asked me if I was English?

We started to chat for a while and Bernard told me that he was from Santa Barbara and was travelling on business. He worked in sales but was looking for other work while travelling.

After some time, I kindly said that I was very pleased to have met him and wished him well, before saying goodbye.

Chapter 2

I arrived at the Anza Hotel in Calabasas on 29 May and walked in on a school reunion. It was extremely busy.

All the travelling had, by now, caught up with me, and I was so tired I went straight in the shower then to bed. I fell asleep instantly, not hearing any of the celebrations from the gathering that night.

There was a choice of breakfast in the morning, continental or cooked. I chose continental as it was warm outside being that it was May.

After breakfast, I decided to go for a walk and get a feel of the area and, perhaps, get chatting to some of the locals before taking on my mission to discuss the Pumpkin Festival.

I was thinking to myself that it was a shame Mr Greaves hadn't waited until October for the story then I could have taken part in the festivities while writing my article.

I took off to the local library to gather some information as to how and when the Pumpkin Festival actually came about.

What an interesting story. It is generally accepted that the name Calabasas is derived from the Spanish *calabaza* meaning 'pumpkin, squash or gourd' (cf. calabash). Some historians hold the theory that Calabasas is derived from the Chumash word *calahoosa* which is said to mean 'where the wild geese fly'.

I found Calabasas to be another of the most interesting places I have ever visited owing to its amazing history. I talked to the local people in the San Fernando Valley, which lies near the Santa Monica Mountains, and I was shown what it would be like had I, indeed, come in October and taken part in the festival.

I had pretty much covered my story in the first five days so I thought I would travel on to Simi for a few days, then return to Calabasas for the remainder of my time.

After my evening meal, I returned to my room to start packing for the next leg of my journey, to the place that I still call home because I have fond memories of my childhood there.

The train took me the twenty-five miles from Calabasas to Simi Valley, through Thousand Oaks on Route 101. It was such a beautiful journey; miles of track with stunning views along the way.

I stayed in the Grand Lodge Hotel and grand it was, with fine smelling flowers on both sides of the entrance.

Again, I unpacked my suitcase, showered and went to sleep for a while, the dry heat, at times, being too much to bear.

Later, I was sitting in the restaurant waiting to order my food when I saw a familiar face. It was Bernard, the man I met back in Canada, and after a minute I could see that he had spotted me too.

I jokingly asked him if he was following me? To which he replied, with a crimson face, "Oh, no not at all. I live in Fernando Valley and I'm on my way back home now. What are you doing here?"

"Well, actually, this is where I was born. I left when I was ten years-old."

"So, what brings you back?" he replied.

"I'm a reporter, I am covering a story in Calabasas and thought while I was here I would visit my roots."

"I thought I knew your face," he said…"I can't think where from but I do know you from somewhere, perhaps we went to the same school?"

"I went to Valley View Junior School?"

"Oh, no, that's not it, I didn't go to that school. Never mind it will come back to me, how long are you visiting Simi?"

"Perhaps a couple of weeks," I said, "I'm not really sure yet."

"Well, maybe I will see you around. I come here often with my work. I hope to see you again."

Once I had finished eating, I took a stroll to see if I could spot anything familiar. Although I remember the house I lived in with my parents, I could only vaguely remember in which area it was as I was so young.

The people of Simi seemed friendly enough and most people that passed me by would say, 'Good evening'. There isn't much of that back in London.

I even saw a familiar face. A woman, probably around my mother's age, I didn't speak to her as she was in the distance and, even if she were closer, I wouldn't have asked if I knew her.

"Beth, Beth, is that you?" I could hear from across the street, as an elderly gentleman got closer. "It is you, Beth McDaid," he said, "Well, I'll be."

The only people to call me Beth are my parents. *Who could this man possibly be?* I thought.

"I was clearing the trash at the back of the restaurant when I caught a glimpse of you," he said. "I wasn't sure at first, but it is you isn't it?"

"Yes, I'm Elizabeth McDaid, do you know me?"

"Why, I was your father's buddy back when we worked at Old Man Tate's cotton field, but you won't remember that, why you must have been around seven at the time."

"I'm sorry, Sir, I don't remember. So, you know my parents?"

"Of course," he said, "I've known your daddy for many years. You all went to London, must be around eleven years ago now?"

"No, Sir, it was twelve. Where are your parents...they here too?"

"No, it's just me, my parents are back in London and doing very well."

"Well, you be sure to tell them I was speaking of them. Tell them things have changed, those dark days are gone. Well, almost."

I carried on walking looking for the house, I should have asked him what he meant by 'those dark days'. In fact, I hadn't even asked his name. I would ask him the next time I saw him.

Only I didn't see him, he passed away two days after he spoke to me. I am sure that I heard some people whisper, "Silly old fool, should have kept quiet."

I was puzzled and I didn't understand what they meant. Walking around those first few days, I attracted some odd looks from the local people and I wondered if it was because they had seen me speaking to the old man.

As I walked across the road my heart was pounding as I saw it; my home, just as I remembered it, only it now lay derelict and the garden looked more than a little overgrown.

I saw a young woman, a couple of years older than me I would say, and she, too, just stood there staring. What was wrong with this place? All of a sudden I felt a little strange. I had a very uneasy feeling, like something wasn't right, although I just couldn't pinpoint what it was.

I gave up and returned to the hotel. I headed straight for the bar, "Gin and tonic please," I said. I needed a drink! I felt like I should not have been there today with so many people staring and one, in particular, pointing at me as she stood there talking to a neighbour.

After my drink, I decided to go to bed. I had had enough for one day. Just as I was about to leave I saw Bernard again.

"Elizabeth," he said, "I have been looking for you."

"Oh, why? You've come a long way just to find me."

"Not really, it's only a short drive away. I know now…"

"Know what?" I asked.

"I know where I have seen you before."

"Where?"

"Remember I said that I knew your face? Yes, but it wasn't your face, well, it was your face but…"

"Oh, Bernard, you are confusing me now and I'm very tired."

"Okay, meet me for breakfast and I will tell you all about it."

"About what?"

"How I recognised you, but it wasn't you, I think it was your sister."

"My what?" I said, "I don't have a sister."

By this time I was very puzzled and extremely tired.

"Of course you do. Your father, his name is Joseph, am I right?"

"Yes, but how do you know that?"

"Elizabeth," he replied, "everyone knows that, the whole valley knows it and the whole story."

"Oh, my Lord above, I'm so tired, I need to sleep."

"Meet me here in the morning for breakfast and I will tell you all about it, let's say 9.00 am sharp."

"Okay, okay, I will meet you, but this better be good because I have had a tough day and all this confusion has exhausted me."

"Goodnight."

Chapter 3

When I awoke the next morning I still felt quite sleepy and I figured it may have been from the events the day before. As much as I was looking forward to meeting Bernard I was thinking that, maybe, this was all a trick, that he had other intentions.

Bernard was already sitting at a table when I walked through the door, and on the table was a beautiful bunch of flowers. That was it! I was convinced he had concocted his story in order to spend time with me again.

"Good morning, Madam," the waiter said as he pulled my chair out on the opposite side of the table.

"Good morning, thank you."

"Would you like iced tea this morning?"

"No thanks, I will just have a glass of water with my breakfast."

"So," I said to Bernard, "What is all this nonsense about my having a sister? I think you are confusing me with someone else I am an only child, I have no siblings."

"Are you sure, Elizabeth? When I told you what school I went to it came back to me that I was in school with someone who looks so much like you, only she has extremely dark hair."

"Bernard, I can assure you, I have no sister and, besides, they say we all have a double somewhere in the world, mine must be right here in Simi.

"While I'm on the subject of Simi, what is it with the people around here? I have been here a few days now and so many people just stare at me, some say 'good day', yet others point their finger like they are gossiping about me?"

"Well, there has been some talk, Elizabeth."

"Talk? Talk of what?"

"You," he said, "I have heard people say, 'That's Bridget McDaid's daughter.'"

"I don't know these people and I'm pretty sure that the old man I spoke to before his death was probably the oldest person here?"

"Well, maybe they are mistaking you for the same person I thought was your sister."

"So, tell me a little about you, I know that you work in sales you mentioned that you attended school here which tells me that you once lived here too?"

"I live in Fernando Valley and, prior to that, I lived right here in Simi, actually not far from here. My parents, along with myself and my brother and sister, moved to Fernando Valley in 1966 as my father figured there would be more opportunity for us children if we moved away. Something happened here in Simi just before we moved but nobody talks about it and if we asked they changed the subject.

"At the time, Santa Susana field laboratory was in operation right up there in the Simi Hills, there was so much noise from rocket testing that some families, including ours, moved elsewhere. We left just before I started senior school, but we still have our home here. My father decided that we should hold on to the property as it would be somewhere to come back to on vacation."

"I see, it sounds fascinating, I imagine it would be very peaceful there now?"

"It is, if you haven't got anything planned I can take you there, it sits around halfway up that hill right over there."

"I can only see one small house from here."

"That's it," he said.

"Wow, I do like the idea of a peaceful location, and I imagine it has some beautiful views from up there."

We arrived at the bottom of the hill and from there it looked like a very steep climb. I was concerned that I was wearing the wrong shoes for such a hike, but Bernard told me not to worry as there was a track and we didn't have to climb.

I couldn't believe my eyes when we reached the ranch, it was stunning from the outside and the views were indeed spectacular.

"You are privileged to have such a wonderful place, and so tastefully decorated," I said to Bernard.

"Yes, we are, now you can see why my father wanted to keep this place."

"I sure can and I would, too, if it were mine. Oh, Bernard, I would give my right arm to live in a ranch like this."

"Why don't you? I know London sounds appealing but it will never be home?"

"No, you're most certainly right there," I said.

Bernard told me to have a look around while he gathered logs for the open fire, ready for the evening.

The ranch was like a giant log cabin once inside, the staircase faced the door as you entered and to one side was the kitchen and a door that led to the log house. I had never seen a kitchen that large. I suppose it had to be for five people and, by the look of Bernard, they needed that space because he was around six feet tall, so I imagined his father and siblings to be equally as tall as he was.

To the back of the kitchen there was a door with a smaller room inside and, as I peeked my head around the door, I could barely see as it was very dark. I could only gather this must have been the pantry.

As I turned around to go through the kitchen Bernard was standing there staring at me with a kettle in his hand, "Tea?"

"Sorry, what?"

"Tea, Elizabeth?"

"Oh, yes, sorry. I'm in awe of how beautiful this place is. I wonder if my old home was like this? I can only remember a little of what it was like, and it feels like it was much smaller."

"No," Bernard said, "they are more or less the same down by, although if you were right in the town it may have been smaller."

After we had had tea, we went for a stroll around the grounds and, at one point, I could just about see the home I lived in further down. Bernard asked me if I would like him to escort me to have a better look.

"Yes, please, I would be grateful, I couldn't really go a few days ago as an old man stopped me and enquired about my father, seems he knew my parents and me when I was a child."

"Ah," said Bernard, "you're talking about old man Quinn. What a character, he did a lot for the people of Simi back in the day, he sure was good to us children when we were young."

"Tell me a little about Mr Quinn, Bernard, I liked him even though I only really chatted to him for a few minutes, he seemed like a wise old man."

"Well, old Quinn lived near Stoney Point Ranch. In fact, he was born here, way back in the day. His parents originated from Italy in the late 1800s. They were farmers, then later opened one of the first Italian sit-in cafes. They were a well-known family and very respected, known later as the 'Italian American's down by'."

"So, what exactly happened to him? I speak to him one day, then two days later he is dead."

"Oh, old age I guess," said Bernard, "he was one of the few remaining old-timers, so to speak. Knew everybody. It didn't matter if they lived in Simi or as far as San Fernando, he knew them and everyone knew him and his family."

I told Bernard that I had overheard people talking about Mr Quinn, and what had happened to him, and asked if he knew what they meant.

"No, I don't, Elizabeth, but it's best you don't ask questions, at least that's what my parents always told me.

"My father would say, 'If you ever go back to Simi don't ask questions about the past.' He would never tell me why. There's nothing stranger than folk is something I always heard my mother say."

Bernard asked me if I would like to go back up to the Ranch for supper after we had visited my old home?

"Of course," I answered, "I would love to."

As we got closer to the house I started to get that old familiar feeling, it was like I was a child again, I could hear laughter in my head, but this time I could see myself on that swing.

"Let's go around the back. I have a feeling there is a large garden there and a couple of swings attached to a tree," I said. And there it was, at the bottom of the garden. The tree had two swings, just as I had imagined. It wasn't as large a garden as I had thought but there was a stream at the bottom with a small wooden bridge.

"So, this is where you lived?" said Bernard, "I remember my parents coming to this house maybe once or twice a week and collecting a crate of eggs."

"Yes, I think that's right. My father was a farmer and this here was the barn but I always thought that it was wooden. It's stone built like the house, only smaller."

"That's right," said Bernard, "it was wooden, but I recall it being burned to the ground and there were lots of people standing around. I could have sworn they were very angry, there was a lot of screaming and shouting, and I remember one or two people fighting."

"So, what was this here?" I asked, pointing to the smaller stone building.

"I'm not sure," Bernard replied. "I don't remember that…what else do you remember?"

"I'm not sure, I was young, and it's not very clear in my head, but I do feel whatever it was it meant trouble and I was upset by the way the adults were fighting."

"I will ask my brother, he is four years older than me and maybe he will know what happened."

As I touched the seat of the swing a flash of memory and a chill came over me. I quickly lifted my hand, which was extremely cold, and tucked it inside my pocket.

Now I didn't feel so good about being there and I didn't know why. Something had happened there and I had the feeling nobody wanted to talk about it.

Chapter 4

Back at the ranch, Bernard lit the log burner, as it was starting to feel a little chilly.

We entered the kitchen while talking about the events of the day. I sat at the large, wooden farmhouse table while he cooked a tasty beef roast with lots of homegrown vegetables, followed by banana nut cake with custard filling.

"Well," I said, "ten out of ten for the chef. That was really good." Bernard smirked like a little shy boy which made me chuckle.

There was a knock on the door. "Who can that be? said Bernard. I watched as he walked towards the door.

"Warren, what are you doing here?" he asked, proceeding to walk outside. I could hear them talking but not what they were saying. Then, all of a sudden, there was a raised voice.

"You should not have brought her here," said Warren.

"Why the hell not? She is visiting her old family home, why wouldn't I bring her here?"

I could just about hear Warren say, "You know you can't encourage her. Don't bring her here again. The past must be left in the past."

I was a little confused, as I was sure it was me they were talking about, but I didn't ask Bernard about what I had heard when he returned inside.

Instead, I asked, "Do you need me to leave Bernard? I think I've taken up enough of your time."

"No," he said, "not at all. That was just Warren, an old friend."

"All the same I think I should go. I feel very tired and, tomorrow, I would like to see a little more of this place before I decide whether to travel or stay longer."

"Stay a little longer," Bernard replied, "I would like to take you out tomorrow and show you around. Can you ride a horse?"

"Well, only once, many years ago, when my parents took me to the country on holiday. To be honest, I would rather walk and take it all in."

"Okay," he said, "What say I meet you after breakfast tomorrow, you can find your way back up here right?"

"Yes, I suppose so, but don't you have to work?"

"No, I have a few days free and I would really like to get to know more about your life in London."

I wasn't in the mood for breakfast. In fact, I really didn't feel too good at all. I had had a nervous kind of feeling since I arrived in Simi and it seemed to be getting worse. It was an odd feeling like something was going to happen, and I hadn't had much sleep. I had woken up at three-thirty in the morning with that damn dream. Since my arrival in Simi, I had kept getting flashbacks, only I still couldn't see the face of the child on the swing. I could see her from the back of her head and she had very long, black hair and was wearing a pink dress with pink shoes.

I have to ask Bernard if he has spoken to his brother yet, I thought, *perhaps he can shed some light on matters or maybe he may know me from when we were children.*

I asked Bernard if his brother could remember anything, but he said that I should be careful asking too many questions.

"Why?" I said to Bernard, "I was born here. It's my home and I have to ask questions so that I can find out if I still have family here."

"My brother said that there weren't really many people left we could ask, except…Well I have a friend whose mom lives in a care home in town. Her memory isn't so good and people say she is not a well woman, but she is the only one I can think of that may recall anything. She is in her 80s, and if anyone would know it would be her."

"Well, what are we waiting for? Let's go there now, I really need to know what is going on around here. I have a feeling people know something about my family but are keeping quiet."

As we approached Simi Residential Home for the Elderly, I was quite shocked by its appearance; the building looked rather rundown, although they kept the garden in good shape with plants and flowers.

Bernard stood at the reception desk waiting for someone to come, he rang the bell a few times but nobody seemed to come to help us.

I was looking at photographs they had on the wall of, what I gathered to be, residents on days out, but one photo, in particular, caught my eye. It was of a little girl holding the hand of a nurse standing by a lake. The funny thing was that the image of the little girl in the photo appeared quite blurry so I couldn't make out her face, but the nurse looked very familiar to me. I heard muffled voices and, as I turned around, I felt my knees start to buckle.

When I came round, I was lying on the floor.

"What happened?" I heard Bernard ask the nurse.

"She passed out, get some water." As I opened my eyes, Bernard and another gentleman were leaning over me.

"What just happened, Bernard?" I asked.

"You fainted, Elizabeth, here drink this water it will make you feel better."

I stood up and looked around and, for a moment, I forgot where I was.

"Is that better?" Bernard asked.

"Yes, I'm not sure why I passed out but the heat in here is just too much." I turned to the photographs on the wall, then I noticed that the photo I had been looking at had disappeared.

I pointed at the wall and said to Bernard, "What happened to...?" I stopped talking. I thought it better not to say anything for now.

"Let's go, Elizabeth, Ms Cassy is in the room down the hall."

As we entered the room, all of a sudden, I felt very cold, an unusual kind of cold, like I had goosebumps all over my body.

"Good morning, Ms Cassy," said Bernard. "It's me, Bernard, Bernard Carter, how are you today? I've brought along an old friend, Elizabeth McDaid."

Just as he said my name, the old woman looked up and her eyes looked right through me. Then she raised her hand and asked me to leave. There was so much coldness in her eyes, it was plain to see she wasn't up to having visitors – or was it just me who she didn't want to see?

Bernard said, "Ms Cassy, it's all right, you don't be scared," but she was having none of it and kicked up such a fuss that the nurse came running through the door and asked us to leave.

"What exactly is going on in this odd little place called Simi Valley?" I asked Bernard. "Something about this place scares me. The little things from my childhood that I can remember fill me with warmth, yet now I feel scared. Something isn't right, someone knows why and I'm going to get to the bottom of it."

That evening I called my parents back home. My mother answered the phone and, when she realised it was me, I could hear the tone in her voice change.

"Mother, I need to know, do you remember old man Quinn and Ms Cassy?" There was complete silence for a few seconds.

"Elizabeth, you need to come home."

"Mother," I said, "please answer me, something is going on here in Simi and I feel like you're keeping something from me."

"Come home, Elizabeth, and I will explain it to you then. Your father is unwell and we really need you right now."

"What is wrong with him?"

"He hasn't been good since you left. He wants you to come home, and the sooner the better."

"Is he so ill that he can't go to work?" I asked her.

"Of course he is still going to work, but he just didn't want you to go back there. We have our reasons and we will explain on your return."

Chapter 5

Of course, I didn't return home. In fact, I extended my trip for another few weeks, which I had to clear with Mr Greaves.

I told him that there were other people who wanted to give their take on the Pumpkin Festival. He told me to take as much time as I needed and, if it took longer than a few weeks, not to worry.

He asked me what I had found out while in Simi.

"How did you know I was in Simi?" I asked him. And what did he mean, 'what I had found out?'

I could hear a woman whispering in the background, "Is she with Bernard?"

"Who is that talking to you, Mr Greaves?"

"Eh, nobody is talking to me."

"But I heard someone ask you if I was with Bernard, how do you know about Bernard?"

"Elizabeth, I will explain everything to you when you come back to London, for now concentrate on Simi. We will speak later." Then he hung up the phone.

Okay, now I knew for sure that something was not right. I proceeded to the hotel to try and get some sleep, having made up my mind to go out the next day and get to the bottom of whatever was going on.

I woke through the night, again sweating from the same dream that was dominating my life, or so it seemed. I paced up and down the room thinking about everything that had happened in this little town since my arrival.

My heart was racing, I felt like I wanted to tear it out, there was so much anger pent up inside of me and this was not like me.

I was staring out of the window and I could see something, or someone, looking up at my window. I didn't know who, all I could see was a dark shadow.

I ran outside but, by the time I got to where they had been standing, they had gone.

It was still very dark outside and I found myself wandering through the trees in the direction of my old home, and there it was, I could see it plain as day. The shadow of the derelict house. What I noticed now that was different from before was that the window at the top of, what was once, the landing was open, and when I was here a few days before it was closed.

Someone had been in the house, but how? There was a fence around it because it was too dangerous to go inside. I stood next to the fence by the bridge trying hard to remember my childhood there. I remembered my mother going to the barn in the morning to collect the eggs and father singing in the bathroom while getting ready to go to work.

I loved breakfast time, when mother would allow me to sit with the home-baked bread on the end of a long fork, in front of the fire, to make toast while she poached the eggs. Then the sound of the chickens outside when someone was coming closer to the house. I remember a man asking mother how she was and chatting about what a fine day it was going to be, Wait…was that old man Quinn? I can see his face but he was much younger…

Mother is handing him a small box filled with eggs. She is smiling at him and he leans toward her, she kisses him…

Father is coming down the stairs. "Elizabeth, what are doing? Elizabeth…"

I'm running away into the barn. The chickens are clucking louder and louder, but I can hear mother and father shouting.

"I was being friendly," Mother shouted.

My father is yelling too, "Get the girls ready for school and we will talk about this when I get home." (The girls? I remember my father saying 'the girls' but I can't remember anyone else being there.)

"Your eggs," Mother shouts after him.

"I'm not hungry, you tell him to stay clear you hear me?"

I can hear banging on the door. "Open the door, Elizabeth, please I know you're in there? Open the door."

I opened my eyes. Sweat was pouring from my face and body. I looked round but I was in my room at the hotel. It was all a dream.

"Elizabeth, what is wrong with you? It's three-thirty in the afternoon. The hotel assumed you were out but you didn't meet me by the house, I have been looking for you everywhere."

I couldn't tell Bernard about the dream, so I told him I wasn't feeling very well.

"Shall we go to the house another day?"

"No," I said, "wait for me downstairs while I get ready."

As we approached the house from the other side of the bridge, I could see just how bad the brickwork was. It was so run down, just the shell remained. It was in pretty bad condition.

I told Bernard that I wanted to go through the fence so that I could go around the back to see how bad it was.

In my mind, I was thinking, *if I buy it I could restore it.*

It was doable, Bernard told me, and right then I decided I would try to find out who owned the house. Maybe it was just a dream but I was sure it was what I wanted.

In the distance we could see someone walking along the bridge but the sun was so strong we could only see a dark shadow.

As the person got closer Bernard called out, "Is that you, Warren?"

Warren called back, "Yes, what are you doing here?"

"Just having a look around," explained Bernard, "this is Elizabeth."

Warren looked at me and proceeded to shake my hand. "So, you're the one everyone in the valley is talking about?"

"Really," I said, "and why would the valley be talking about me?"

"Oh, you know, the girl from the past…that's what I hear them saying, seems there are a few people who don't want you here."

"Maybe that's because I'm a journalist, who knows, but I guess if they are talking about me they are leaving someone else alone, right?"

Warren decided to stick around and walked with us around the old place. He said, "You know, this old place could be made to look good again. I remember, as a child, wishing I lived in a home like this. My parents lived over there…" He pointed across the river, "Our home was a little old wooden shack which is long gone."

"Well," I said to him, "I think I may just bring the house back to its former glory."

"You mean you're actually going to buy this place?"

"Yes," I said, "Why not? It was my home."

"So, do you plan to move back here from London?" Warren asked.

"Yep! I may just do that."

"Then you're a very brave woman, because I wouldn't live here, not after what happened."

"What do you mean, after what happened? There seems to be a lot of whispering about me and this old home of mine, yet nobody seems to want to tell me exactly what's going on. When I ask they say the past is best left in the past but I think it is about time I found out the truth."

Chapter 6

I went to the local library to see if I could find out who owned the old house, and the lady there said she would make a few phone calls to the Planning Division of the City Council.

It turned out that the house was owned by a gentleman back in England but they were unable to give me his details, they said they could make a call and express my interest.

So, that was that, I would know within a week or so if he was interested in selling and how much he wanted for the property.

By now Bernard and I had spent quite some time together so it was no surprise to me that, on the few days I had on my own while he was away working, I found I missed his company.

I had rented a small cottage for the remainder of my time in Simi, as I had extended my stay again, and it made more sense to leave the hotel and have my own space.

I was in the grocery shop buying supplies when a woman came to the counter with her husband. She looked me up and down, then said to me, "So, you're the one?"

"I beg your pardon," I replied.

"You're the daughter of Joe and Bridget McDaid?"

"Yes, I am," I said, "do you know my parents?"

"Oh, yes, I do. In fact, we all do. So, what brings you back to Simi?"

"Work," I told her, "I'm a journalist. I had a story to cover in Calabasas and decided to visit my childhood home while I am here."

"I see, and have you been to visit your aunt yet?"

"My aunt? I wasn't aware that I still had relatives here."

She held out her hand to shake mine and said, "My name is Rebecca, and this is my husband, Clint."

"Very nice to meet you both," I replied. Rebecca invited me to their home for breakfast. I tried to make excuses but she wouldn't take no for an answer.

Her home was beautiful. It was a much bigger ranch than Bernard's, with a barn full of chickens and a stable where Rebecca kept her horses.

"So," she said, "you didn't know that you have family here?"

"No, I didn't."

"Well, your Aunt Cassy still lives here, although she is very frail now, then there is Mark, her son."

"Hold on, the lady I briefly met at the residential home? Bernard introduced her to me, Ms Cassy he said her name was."

"That's her, she is your aunt. I think she is your father's aunt, actually. I'm not sure but I know she is a member of your family."

"What about Mark?" I asked. "He is her son, you say, so where can I find him?"

"He moved away years ago to Bakersfield. After what happened he thought it best to make a fresh start and move away. He never visits your aunt, you know, I think he has been only once about five years ago."

"Tell me, Rebecca," I said, "what exactly is it that nobody wants to talk about? All I know is there is some kind of secret and all I hear is, 'the past should be left in the past!'"

"You mean you don't know?" asked Rebecca.

"I don't know anything, that's why I'm asking you."

"There was a fire years ago and they say it was started deliberately. Then there was an affair that caused a scandal."

"Okay, what fire and what affair?" I enquired curiously.

"I remember my parents talking in the kitchen about old Quinn, he was your uncle," she said. "He had no business doing what he did to Ms Cassy, and if it hadn't happened then the fire in the barn would not have been started. They say it was lucky that you all got out and that the fire was put out before any real damage was done to the house, but the barn was completely ruined."

"Wait, so that happened in my home? I don't remember any of this."

"Well, you wouldn't, you were only a nipper. I do remember the fire. There were a lot of people gathered around and a fight broke out between old man Quinn and, I think, your father."

Right then, I decided that, as soon as I knew about the house, I would fly back to London for answers.

I met up with Bernard on his return, as we had arranged to go for lunch.

"Bernard," I said, "we need to talk. I'm confused about what happened here when I was a child."

"What do you mean?" he replied.

"Well, while you have been away I met a lady called Rebecca. She told me a little about the fire at my parents' barn, and that old man Quinn was my uncle. She also told me that his wife, Ms Cassy, is my aunt. What's going on?"

"I'm not sure," said Bernard. "I didn't know she was your aunt, but I will help you to find out what went on."

The lady from the library called me to go and see her about the house. "Well," she said. "It's good news. Mr McDaid would, indeed, like to sell the property."

"Mr McDaid?" I repeated.

"Yes, the property division contacted me to say that he is happy to sell the property but he wants a fair price for it. They need you to go to their office in the city to discuss it further."

The penny dropped, and I thought to myself, *my father must still own the property but why has he held on to something that he walked away from all those years ago?*

I went along to the property division offices in the city and spoke with a Mr Carter who had all the details ready for me to look over.

"Now then," he said, "you understand that this property is in need of a lot of repair?"

"Yes," I replied, "I want to get all the figures before I commit to buying. Can you give me some background history on the property?"

"Yes, hold on while I show you something."

"Here it is," he said, "this is a copy of an old real estate valuation report of the property. Back then the owner took over the mortgage from his parents who owned the house prior to him. It cost his parents $380 to buy, but by the time they passed away it was worth $6,900 and the owner, Mr McDaid, took it over. By 1960 he owned it outright."

"Okay, so he is still the owner, right?"

"Yes, he moved to England back in 1962. I believe he put the house on the market but, due to the fire damage in the barn, and a little to the house, there were no buyers."

"So he took it off the market and kept hold of it I guess?"

"Yes," said Mr Carter. "My colleague has spoken to the owner and he is willing to sell. We have advised him that, due to its current condition, he will probably only get around $16,500 and he is happy to go with that."

Sounds good to me, I thought. I had enough saving for the deposit, so I told him I was interested but I had one rule before I would commit to buying.

"I must remain anonymous at all costs, I do not want the seller to know my name or anything about me."

"Okay, I'm pretty sure we can do that so shall we draw up the contract and get to work?"

"Absolutely," I told him, and that was that! He said it would take a couple of weeks to get the paperwork ready then they would call me to sign the contract.

Chapter 7

I told Bernard I was going back home as I needed to sort things out, and that I would be back within the month.

Before I left, I asked him to take me back to visit Ms Cassy. I wanted to see what else I could find out before returning home. We arranged to go see her again the next day.

Meanwhile, I went back to see Rebecca. I told her that I wanted her to speak with her parents and try to find out what happened on the night of the fire. I pretty much begged her not to fall for all this 'the past is better left in the past' nonsense.

She said she would do her best, then I went to talk to Warren and asked him to do the same.

Bernard was acting a little strange and asked me not to speak to his brother.

"Why?" I asked him. As he was a few years older, he would probably know more than most.

Bernard said that we really needed to talk, before I asked anyone else any questions, and he offered to cook me dinner that evening at his old family home.

As I was getting ready I looked out of the cottage window. On the roadside I could see a young woman with long black hair staring at the cottage, a blank expression on her face. She looked familiar and I tried to open the window to see her more clearly, but she started to walk in the direction of the trees opposite.

Something told me that she was there for a reason, so I left the cottage and tried to follow her. Then, as I crossed the road towards the trees she started to walk faster in the direction of the old house.

Then the rain came, it was very heavy and I was soaked by the time I reached the old wooden bridge, along from the house. I could see the young woman standing in front, staring blankly.

I called out to her, "Hey, are you lost?" She moved to the other side of the house, and by the time I got there she was gone. It was late, I was soaked and I should have been at Bernard's an hour ago.

When I turned up, he asked, "Where have you been? Look at you, you're dripping wet."

"I know," I said, "but you won't believe what has happened."

I started to tell Bernard the whole story about the dream back in the hotel and what had just occurred.

"Elizabeth, there is something I need to tell you, it's about your sister."

"Oh, not this again," I said, "I don't have a sister."

But he carried on talking. "Elizabeth, you do have a sister. She is the daughter of old man Quinn." Now, I really was confused.

"Bernard, you need to tell me what's going on, I have a sister? Are you sure?"

"Yes, it seems that your mother and old man Quinn had an affair, and out of that affair your mother had a daughter."

"I don't know what you're talking about Bernard. I'm sure that if I had a sister she would have grown up with me right? And my parents have never told me anything about this. Are you certain?"

"Yes, and I already knew about you before I met you."

"How? I don't get it."

"Well," he said, "I have a colleague who knows you and asked me to track you down. She is the wife of Ms Cassy's son."

"So, you know that Ms Cassy is my aunt?"

"Well, I didn't until recently."

"I'm going to visit her again," I said. "I want to know exactly what she knows." Bernard thought it best I take things slowly and reminded me that Ms Cassy was in a fragile state.

When the day of the visit came, I was a little nervous in case she started shouting again, it was obvious by now that she knew me.

She was a little anxious when I first entered the room, then she asked, "Is that you, Lily?"

I spoke to her in a calm voice so as not to upset her. "No, Ms Cassy, I'm Elizabeth."

46

"Little Beth?"

"Yes, that's right. My parents call me Beth. You know my parents, Joe and Bridget?"

She looked at me with a squint in her eye and said, "You're that child."

"What child?" I asked?

"You're Lily's sister."

I asked her who Lily was and I was shocked when she answered, "You don't know your own sister, do you?"

I couldn't get any more from her. She became uneasy and shouted for the nurse. I asked the nurse if I could wait until Ms Cassy calmed down but she said it was best that I go.

Before leaving the room, I asked her, "Are you my aunt?"

She turned to me with a look of horror on her face and said, "Indeed I am not."

Chapter 8

I arrived back home in London just before my father got home from work. My mother was happy to see me. She asked me how my trip was, and I told her it was extremely informative, so much so I had some questions that needed answering.

"Yes," she said, "I thought you would." I asked her about Ms Cassy and told her that people said she was my aunt and that old man Quinn, who had passed away a few days after I arrived, was her husband.

My mother told me that Ms Cassy was actually my father's aunt and her husband was, indeed, Mr Quinn. Then she added that she didn't think she was still alive because she had been carted off to hospital due to losing her mind.

"What do you mean, she lost her mind, what happened to her?"

"We don't know. One moment she was fine, then all of a sudden she went crazy and they took her to the hospital."

My mother went on to tell me that it was the talk of the valley when Ms Cassy married Mr Quinn because he was so much younger than her. "Maybe she just couldn't handle being the talk of the place," she said.

I was about to ask my mother about Lily but decided I would keep quiet for now. I wanted to see if she might tell me herself.

I told her that I went to see the house, but it was pretty much a ruin, and I told her that there wasn't much left of the barn. I said that people had told me it had caught fire. Then I asked her what had happened.

Her expression changed. She told me that my father was smoking a cigarette, which he thought he had put out but, in fact, it caused the fire in the barn.

Now, I knew for sure she was lying and I didn't ask her anything else. I wanted to buy the house and couldn't ask any more questions or they might realise that I was the buyer.

Dad came in, just in time for dinner. I don't think he was expecting me to be home until later that evening. He looked at me and nodded. I asked him how his day had been and he replied, "No different from any other."

"How was your trip?" he asked.

"It went well," I said. "I wrote my story about the Calabasas Pumpkin Festival, but I'm planning another trip in October as a follow up."

"Very good," he said.

Then my mother said to him, "Beth was asking me about your aunt Cassy."

My father turned around, "What do you want to know? I would prefer you don't know too much about her. She went mad and was admitted to hospital. I haven't seen her for years and don't intend to see her again. How did you find out about her anyway? Your mother and I have never discussed her."

"Some people from the valley told me that she was my aunt and that she was in a residential home."

"Did you visit her by any chance?" he asked.

"No, I didn't. I'm not sure she would know me, as I don't remember her."

"Well, best to keep it that way."

I went into work the next morning and Mr Greaves summoned me to his office. There was a man with him who introduced himself as Mark Quinn. Mr Greaves said that Mark and I had something to talk about and left the room.

Mark shook my hand and said, "Elizabeth, I have been looking for you for a number of years." He then went on to tell me the full story.

It turns out that his sister, Lily, is my twin. Mark explained that my mother and his father had an affair. My mother fell pregnant and she had twins.

I was shocked and asked him why I hadn't known about this and why was Lily not here in London with me. He said that my father was so angry that he refused to acknowledge the children. He told my mother she had to choose; either she give up the twins or the marriage was over.

The argument went on for months.

"At one point," he said, "your father left your mother then came back but he stood his ground. My mother came up with the idea that she take one of you, and your mother the other.

"Then what happened?" I asked.

"Well, he took some persuading but in the end your father agreed, but not before he went crazy. He found my father and your mother in the barn together."

"So, the affair continued," I asked?

"Yes, for a very long time, I believe."

"Then what?" I asked.

"Well, a huge fight broke out. He set fire to the barn and said he would set fire to the house too. He tried to destroy everything and some damage was sustained to the house. Your mother and father went to stay at the Grand Lodge Hotel until the house was fit to go back to, but they never did.

"Your father put the house up for sale and told my mother that he was moving away, he couldn't cope with the fact that everyone in the valley knew what had happened. I guess he thought that by moving away the whole thing would be forgotten and they could make a fresh start.

"My mother told me the whole story when I was younger. Then a couple of years later the guilt was too much for her so my father and she got divorced. That's when she changed.

"She wasn't a good mother to Lily, so much so that she put her up for adoption. I tried to find her for a long time and when I did it was too late."

"Why was it too late?" I asked.

"She discovered the truth and, together with the fact that she was adopted to an abusive father, she committed suicide. That's when I decided to try and find you, I knew that you went to England, so I hired a private detective."

"That explains the young lady I saw at the hotel. Did Lily have long black hair?"

"Yes," Mark said, "you weren't identical twins but you both looked very much alike."

I told Mark that I had spoken to Mr Quinn before he passed away and that he told me he knew me and my parents. Also, that he said to tell my parents that those dark days were gone.

Mark explained, "I stopped talking to my father after my mother told me what happened."

"Now I understand what Mr Quinn was referring too, and why I kept having that dream."

"What dream?" Mark asked.

"Well, I vaguely remember sitting on the swing at the back of the house. There was another girl on the other swing but I could never see her face. I always wondered who she was."

"That would have been Lily, she played on the swing with you sometimes when your father was at work. Mind, your mother never did tell your father she had been there. When he did find out, things started to go wrong. I guess he couldn't cope with having both of you around; it just reminded him of all that had happened."

Mark said he was returning to Bakersfield in a few days but would love for me to come visit him when I go back to buy the house.

I asked him, "How did you know I am buying the house?"

"Bernard is one of my closest friends. He was in on my plan to find you, but please don't be angry, I made him promise not to tell you anything because I wanted to tell you myself. After all, you're my half-sister and discovering that Lily is dead made me want to find you even more."

"Mark, I have to ask, someone was watching me at the cottage I rented, did you have anything to do with that? Funnily enough, she looked very familiar."

"No," Mark said, "I didn't have anyone watching you other than Bernard and the private detective."

Chapter 9

I went home from work in a foul mood and now I couldn't hold back what I knew. I wanted answers.

My parents were in total shock when I told them I knew about Lily, then an argument broke out. My father was about to storm off but I stood in front of the door.

"Now do you see?" he said to my mother, "I told you this would come back to haunt us." My mother couldn't speak. She stood there with her mouth wide open.

After a short time, she burst into tears, "I want my Lily," she repeated three times. My father looked at her with disgust.

I told them not to bother filling me in, as I knew everything I had to know, and I would never forgive them for keeping this from me.

"I am going back to Simi," I told them. My mother said she wanted to come too, she said she wanted to see Lily. I screamed at her and told her that Lily was dead.

Breakfast was on the table next morning but I struggled to eat. My father had already left for work so it gave my mother the freedom to tell me exactly what had happened.

She more or less told me, just as Mark had explained it, but she also told me that she and Mr Quinn had actually dated prior to her marrying my father.

She said to me, "Beth, Frank – Mr Quinn, and I loved each other very much but my father didn't approve and told me I had to marry your father because he could provide for me and he was a hardworking man. Frank was a drinker and didn't hold out much hope of being a good husband.

"So, I married your father but Frank and I still saw each other when we had the chance. I know that it was wrong but he and I thought that, one day, we could be together."

I asked my mother, "How on earth could you think that when you were already married?"

"Well, I didn't plan on staying married to your father and, deep down, he knew that I could never love him the way I did Frank Quinn."

"And do you still love Frank Quinn?" I asked her.

"Yes," she said.

"You do know that he is dead?"

Right there she broke down in tears. "Yes, I received a letter from an old friend who told me he had died. She also told me that you were in Simi."

I understood, once my mother had explained everything that had happened, and I forgave her, but I told her that I could never forgive my father for making her choose, or for bringing us to London.

I also told her that I was planning on going back to Simi, possibly for good. She wept and hugged me. She said, "You know that if it's what you want to do, I won't try to stop you."

I asked her what she would do now and she said she would be fine, and not to worry. "Your father and I will be okay, he will calm down eventually, but don't think that he doesn't love you. Maybe, at first, he didn't but as the years went by, he became very fond of you."

At work, I spoke to Mr Greaves and, without going into too much detail, I explained that I had to go back to Simi. I also asked him why he hadn't told me that Mark was looking for me.

He said that Mark had hired a private investigator who made him promise not to tell me and that he should send me to Calabasas to do a story so that he could contact me there. Then, when he went to find me, I had already left for Simi, that's where Bernard came in.

Mr Greaves understood my situation and told me not to worry, that my job it would remain open until I decided what my long-term plans were.

So, with that, I shook his hand and thanked him for everything he had done for me. He added that, should I decide to stay in Simi, he would give me a good reference if I needed it.

My mother cried as I packed my things to go back to Simi. I told her that I would write regularly and I would send her money, once I found a job.

She replied, "I don't need it. I have plenty of money that I had been saving for a rainy day." She said that Frank Quinn had been sending her regular cheques since we left, right up until I was sixteen. (Now I understood why she had been receiving mail from the USA on a regular basis.)

I asked her if my father knew about this. She said, "No, and he never will."

So that was our secret. She then said, "You leave in two days' time. I will withdraw all of the money for you."

I refused. "That is your money," I said, "keep it." But she wouldn't have it, saying it was for me and that it would be a good start to a new life.

Two months after I arrived back in Simi, my mother passed away. They said it was natural causes but I think it was from a broken heart. Not only had she lost Frank Quinn, the love of her life, but she knew she would never have Lily in her life.

I'm glad now that I took the money, I wouldn't have wanted my father to be left with it, not after what he did. He broke my mother's heart and I never spoke to him again.

Chapter 10

"I fixed the old house up good and proper, Bernard, what do you think?"

"Yep, you sure did," he said, "it's looking great."

"How about dinner next week when I have finished the furnishings?"

"You bet, I can't wait to try your cooking."

I bought myself an old typewriter and some supplies with a view to writing my manuscript. I was working part time in the Planning Division of the City Council and my job was to visit old properties and evaluate if they could be repaired and what the cost would be.

It wasn't long before Mark came to visit me and we talked at length about the future, he asked me if I was interested in Bernard and, of course, I was, as was Bernard in me but we were taking it slowly. I still had a lot on my mind regarding Lily.

I asked Mark if he had been to see his mother, and he said, "No."

"Well, I think you should," I said. "I also think you should forgive her, as I forgave my mother, and now she is no longer here. It's only a matter of time and your mother will be gone too."

So, he agreed, but he said he wanted me to come with him.

The next day I was taking a walk through the woods and, in the distance, I could see the woman again; the one with the long black hair. I called out to her but she disappeared.

I couldn't understand why I was seeing her all the time, nor why she kept disappearing?

I started to think that I, too, was losing my mind, until I went with Mark to visit Ms Cassy, who looked astonished when she saw us both.

"Mother," Mark said to her, and she looked at him with a smile.

"Mark, you haven't visited me in such a long time."

"I know," he said to her, "I'm sorry, but I'm here now."

Ms Cassy looked at me and said, "You have brought Lily with you."

"No," Mark corrected, "This is Elizabeth, Lily's sister, she knows, Mother, I have told her everything."

I told Mark that I was going out to reception for some tea and I would leave them to talk.

"All right," he said, "I won't be too long."

I was sitting, drinking my tea, when I remembered about the photograph of the nurse and the young girl by the lake. One of the nurses came over and sat down beside me, as I looked at the board. The photo was there again, and I asked the nurse who it was.

"That's Ms Cassy and her daughter."

"Ms Cassy, as in that 'Ms Cassy'" I asked?

"Yes, she was a nurse here many years ago. That is her daughter, Lily."

"I didn't know that she was a nurse."

"Yes, she worked here for many years. Everyone loved her but she took ill and ended up coming here as a resident. That photograph was taken on one of our days out when we could bring our children with us."

The day after Mark and I visited Ms Cassy she passed away. Mark was pretty distraught and it broke his heart that it took me telling him to go and see her and to forgive her.

Bernard and I were having dinner. It was a beautiful evening; there was a rainbow in the sky, although it was chilly. We were sitting by the fire when I heard a noise outside. I went to the window and stood there frozen.

I had repaired the ropes on the old swings by the tree. It was my only happy memory and I wanted to restore that too. There was someone on the swing. I said to Bernard, "Come quickly, there is that woman I keep seeing, sitting on the swing."

I ran out to the swings so that she couldn't get away again and, as she turned around, I realised that it was her; Lily.

She hadn't died? I didn't understand. Mark had said that she committed suicide. But here she was sitting on the swing.

It wasn't a dream. She looked at me and said, "Elizabeth, I knew you would come back."

"I thought you were dead. Mark said you were dead."

She started to cry. "Your father, Joe, wanted me out of your life, he wanted me dead. I came looking for you, I came to your home, but your father told me to go and never come back. He said it would kill our mother if she knew I was there. He made me leave and I had nowhere to go. I was homeless so he paid me to leave."

"But Mark said that you committed suicide."

"My mother told him that, she said that she was sent a letter from my adopted parents.

"I had nothing left, Elizabeth. Only you, and I waited and waited. I visited you in your sleep and hoped you would remember sitting on the swing beside me. Now you are home, here with me, and I can finally be at peace."

I stood as the tears ran down my face...

Epilogue

It's been five years since I came back to Simi and I am now married to Bernard and with our very own twins.

The good thing to come out of all this is knowing that my mother went to her grave guilt free, because she no longer had to keep her secret, and she is now with the love of her life, Frank Quinn, and Lily, my sister.

It broke my heart that it was all a dream, that Lily wasn't really still alive. Some say that Lily came to me so that I would know of her. Mark was lucky to have known Lily before she killed herself, and he said to me that she was finally free from the horrible childhood and past that she had had.

That swing is still attached to the tree and remains empty. Until our own girls can sit there, as I once did with Lily, it will continue to leave a void in my life. In the meantime, it is a reminder of the sister I lost, now at peace, but remembered always.

About the Author

Belinda Conniss is an author and novelist who has published two autobiographical books and a book of poetry. *The Empty Swing* is the first of many fictional short stories.

The author regularly blogs about celebrities, events, food, travel and much more.

In her spare time, Belinda enjoys theatre, writes articles on many subjects, promotes many individuals and enjoys photography.

You will find Belinda on Twitter: @balou5 and on Facebook: @belindaconnissauthor.

Belinda's books are available from www.amazon.co.uk, www.amazon.com and www.barnesandnoble.com online shop, both in print and on Kindle.

Belinda Conniss

Also by this author:

Sad, Lonely & A Long Way From Home
Secrets & Lies
Tears On My Pillow

www.insideoutlastyle.com

Printed in Great Britain
by Amazon